THE DARE

AVA STONE

DEDICATION

To Ryan, for believing in my writing and encouraging me to publish my first book. Your unrelenting love for me is what keeps me going.

PROLOGUE

I COULD SMELL the wet concrete, the dank, dark sky above me, promising another downpour, and soon. I quickened my pace to try to beat the rain, and my mom, to the house. I was soaking wet, and muddy. I didn't want to have to explain to her the reason why.

At least the job was done, for now. Unless someone went digging and made the discovery.

I can't believe this all started out with a dare.

CHAPTER ONE

NOW

"So, after twenty years, you're confessing? You're telling us the whole true story this time?" Detective John Miller asked, taking his seat in the white-walled, brightly-lit room.

"I think it's finally time. I can't live with this any longer," Neve Anderson replied, already seated across the table from Detective Miller. "Just be quiet and let me start from the beginning."

Neve sat back in her chair, folding her left leg over her right. Her hands folded neatly in her lap. "It's going to be a long, insane story."

Then

It was a cold October night, and we were bored. Rather than sitting in my friend Courtney's basement watching more old horror movies, we decided to go explore the woods behind the Kitney playground. She had spent all day trying to convince me to go, that it would be fun, so I finally agreed.

I really had no choice in agreeing to go. Courtney wasn't one to take no for an answer. She always got what she wanted. She was relentless. But I had no other plans, or any other friends to hang out with. It had always been me and Courtney, and up until recently, our friend, Jeremy. *What could be more fun than a real-life ghost-hunting or paranormal hunting adventure, right?*

"It beats watching these predictable movies," Courtney said. "And come on Neve, we need a real experience."

She was right, I was bored and wanted to do this, but it didn't mean that I wasn't slightly nervous about it, too.

Things had been so dull lately and watching the same old slasher flicks just wasn't that fun anymore. She was my best friend, and she wasn't an *awful* person, so if I said no, she wouldn't be mad, but she'd definitely have gone without me. I couldn't just let her go into the woods by herself.

Little did I know what was to come of our spontaneous adventure, that our night would become my worst nightmare.

***

The woods that night were lit by the unusually bright moon. The air was crisp and calm. Courtney guided us through the woods, her long golden locks of hair glimmering over her plaid coat.

"Wait up," I called, trying to match pace with her long strides. Courtney was much taller than me, and I swore power walking was her favorite sport, especially when I was tagging along.

"Was I walking too fast again?" She frowned, eyeing my legs. "You really should've stretched, you know."

Thanks for the constant reminder, Courtney. Letting out a humph, we continued embracing the woods.

Courtney loved reminding me that I was much shorter than her and most people even. It was my biggest insecurity, and I hated being reminded of it. But that's what Courtney was good at, boosting her own ego while bringing everyone around her down, always making sure that her perfections shined the brightest.

A few more paces into our journey, Courtney abruptly stopped, putting her hand out next to her head to signal for me to stop me as well.

"What? Why did you stop walking?" I huffed, out of breath from keeping up with her and nervous as to her reasoning for why she stopped so suddenly.

She turned her head towards me with her index finger over her lips, gesturing for me to be quiet. She listened for a little bit then whispered, "I heard something."

We stood there on the path, still as statues, listening. I forced myself to steady my breathing. I could feel the little hairs all over my body rise from goosebumps. I was easily scared, especially when I was outside in the dark, where there were no other people – at least that I knew of. Then I heard rustling from the path ahead of us. It was too far off to see what, or who, was making the noise.

"It's probably just an animal," I suggested, because that was the most rational, non-horrifying possibility. *Please don't let it be anything other than an animal.*

Courtney shook her head. She grabbed my arm and

pulled me from the path and behind a thick trunk of a massive tree. *Is this her way of hiding us?*

The rustling noise continued, seemingly getting closer. It sounded like heavy footsteps, too heavy to be any animal that would be in Kitney.

My heart thudded, and if Courtney heard it, she didn't let on. Looking at her, I could tell she was scared, too. That did nothing to calm my nerves though. Courtney was always the braver of the two of us, and if she was scared, I couldn't help but be full-on panicked.

We stood there behind that tree listening for a while. The footsteps seemed to have gone in a different direction because they began to fade. We waited a few seconds and then made our way back to the main path once we were sure whoever or whatever was out there was completely gone.

"Probably just an animal, huh?" Courtney asked, looking at me in a way that let me know she thought I was crazy, but her expression still showed hints of nervousness.

"Or other kids out like us," I offered, smiling weakly, knowing I was scared to be out here in the dark. "We definitely aren't the only ones out here looking for an adventure." I laughed, trying to lighten the mood and lessen my fear.

"Let's keep going," she said as she started walking along the path again. "I wonder if there are any wolves or anything out here."

"I doubt it, these woods are just as boring as Kitney," I said.

And it was true. Up until that night, nothing crazy bad has ever happened in the dull town of Kitney. The two most exciting things to ever happen in our town were the local gas station getting robbed for ten dollars and a classmate of ours that was reported as missing the previous week, but we all just thought she just ran away.

"I don't even think these woods have ghosts."

"I don't know," Courtney said, smiling mischievously, "Has anyone ever explored out here? Like really explored? I mean every town has some kind of ghost, Neve."

"Not Kitney." That was true. There were no ghost stories, no haunted house or old folklore surrounding our small town.

We continued, freaking ourselves out over every movement or noise that hadn't come from us, then laughing at how freaked out we were over something that probably was an animal that time.

It wasn't long until we were standing face to face with what would become our worst nightmare thus far in our fourteen years of life.

CHAPTER TWO

"WHOA, WHO LIVES HERE?" Courtney asked in awe, as she pulled out her phone. She opened the camera. "Here, take my picture in front of this creepy beauty." She handed me her phone and went and posed in front of the creepy, shabby house we had discovered.

"I think the correct question would be 'Who lived here?', because I'm thinking this is abandoned."

"You think?" She grabbed her phone back, flipped it to selfie mode, then pushed and positioned me so that we could take a selfie together. I smiled as she proceeded with the photos. It was such a fake smile because I was so nervous being in front of this house.

"Well, let's find out," Courtney said excitedly.

She has way too much energy, way more than I do.

I did have to admit that I was somewhat excited too. I mean it definitely wasn't every day that we found something interesting and potentially abandoned here. And anything we discovered would give us exciting stories to tell later at school. Plus, if the place really was abandoned,

I knew it would make the best high school hangout. After all, no one knew about it. If any kid at our school had had knowledge of this place, we'd know.

I walked up to the door, the wooden porch squeaky under my feet and knocked as loudly as I could. I then turned around and gave Courtney a thumbs up, smiling long enough for her to take photographic documentation, again. *This girl and her pictures.*

I knocked again, and when still no one had opened the door, we knew that was our confirmation that the place was abandoned. Along with the fact that no lights were on anywhere, and the condition of the house was horrible, we concluded that no one had been there in a very long time to care for the place.

"I think we have an abandoned house to explore," I said, grabbing the doorknob and twisting. Courtney ran up behind me. "It's locked though, so let's find another way in."

We walked around to the back of the house, but that door was locked too.

We looked at each other and Courtney looked up, pointing and said, "Ohhh, windows, let's try the windows!"

As far as we could see all around the house, no windows were broken and the ones we were able to reach were locked. *If this house is abandoned, why was everything locked?* That was when we discovered it.

There was a basement door on the side of the house. The door itself was closed, but the lock latch was open. Walking up to the door, I turned the knob and gently pulled, causing the door to crack open.

We looked at each other excitedly, mouths gaping open. "I dare you to go in," Courtney said with a giggle.

"Are you serious?" I laughed. "Are you daring me?"

"Yes," she said. "I am." We both laughed.

"I'll go first, but you have to come with." I poked her shoulder. "No way am I going down there myself."

We both stood in the threshold of the open basement door, staring into the darkness. After a long deep breath, I took the first step in. It was completely black as far as I could see. I ran my gloved hands along either side of the wall, feeling for a light switch. Finally, I pulled my phone out of my back pocket and switched on the flashlight. *Why didn't I think of this to begin with?*

I began walking down the stairs. They were dirty with thick layers of muddy footprints. *Are those fresh?* The air was cool and smelled of mildew and decay. As we neared the bottom, the rotten smell got stronger, making my stomach turn.

"I think I smell dead rats," I whispered.

At the bottom, we discovered a chain for the single light bulb on the ceiling. Once the basement was lit up, I turned off my flashlight on my phone and we began to explore. I pulled on the gloves I'd brought in case we found something worth exploring. No way was I going to let all this grungy crap dirty my hands up.

At first, it seemed to be just a regular old basement, filled with boxes and large storage containers. Shelves that were lined with old cans and jars of preserves. But then, I found a small wooden box I wanted to look at a little closer, but I couldn't get it open with my gloves on. I pulled them off and tossed them onto another box, one fell to the floor, but I hardly noticed.

Nothing else special stood out until we neared the darkened back corner behind a large stack of heavy boxes.

Until we discovered where the smell emanated from.

CHAPTER THREE

CHAINED TO A THICK, slightly rusted water pipe, was a decaying body. It looked to be a female. Although we were not a professional forensics team, we knew that the body had been there for quite some time. Or at least it seemed that way to us. There was something about her that was familiar, but her body was covered in so much mud and dried blood it was hard to be certain. *Who is she?*

I thought that my first reaction to a real-life dead body would be to scream, but that wasn't my reaction at all. In fact, the last thing I was able to do was scream.

My stomach instantly lurched, and it took everything in me not to projectile vomit the remainder of cold pizza I had eaten for dinner just a few hours earlier.

Courtney let out a disgusted squeal and bolted faster than I had ever seen her run. I soon followed her back up the stairs and out into the fresh cool air. *It really did smell rancid down there.*

"What the actual hell!" Courtney screamed.

I couldn't speak. I feared that if I tried, I would vomit. I just stood there, silent, waiting for the sick feeling to go away.

When I finally could speak, I said, "Should we call the cops? We should totally call the cops."

"What if we get arrested?" Courtney said.

"Why would we get arrested?" I asked.

"We went down there, touched everything. Our fingerprints will be everywhere." Courtney paced in small circles. "We'd go down for this."

"If our fingerprints are down there, the killer's prints will be too," I said.

"Yeah, but killers are, like, good. They know how to remove their prints. They probably wore gloves anyway."

"Okay," I said, trying to think quickly. I added, "Then let's go remove our prints, wipe them off everything."

"Do you remember everything you touched?" Courtney asked, rudely. "And it'll take so long, what if the killer comes back then kills us? I'm not going back down there."

"Then maybe we should just leave, pretend like this never happened," I offered.

"I don't think I'll ever forget that smell or what happened here." Courtney cringed. "But you're right, let's just get out of here."

Following behind Courtney, we started walking back from the way we came. I was shaking, but I couldn't tell if she was too. The image of the dead girl kept flashing through my mind, and the awful smell lingered in my nose.

I reached to scratch the side of my face when I realized

I was missing my gloves. I forgot to grab them in our hurry to get the hell out of there.

"Oh, no!" I exclaimed.

Courtney spun around so fast asking, "What?"

CHAPTER FOUR

"MY GLOVES," I said. "Crap, I left them down there."

"NO!" Courtney shouted. "No, we have to get them. If we just leave them and the killer comes back, he'll know we were down there and that we know."

We both took off running, as fast as we could, back to the house.

The door was still open when we arrived. I couldn't remember if we had shut it or not, but at that agonizing moment, I didn't even question it. I just wanted to get my gloves and get the hell out of there as fast as I could.

Pausing at the top of the stairs for a brief moment, we both gave each other a look that told the other 'let's do this'. We ran back down into the basement with me in the lead and Courtney trailing very close behind. The stairs were still dark, but we noticed the light at the bottom was still shining. The foul odor we smelled previously was still there, but because of my adrenaline, this time it didn't bother me.

Once we stepped into the lighted area, I immediately

saw my gloves. One was hanging off the top of a box, the other on the cold concrete floor.

Before going back up, I flipped on my phone flashlight to use as guidance rather than the basement light and pulled the chain to turn off the hanging light. I had wanted as little evidence as possible that we were there.

"Good idea," Courtney murmured.

We went back up a little more slowly this time. I kept my head on a swivel, looking all around me and shining my phone in all directions. That's when I noticed it. The one thing that could potentially ruin our plans of just leaving and forgetting everything.

CHAPTER FIVE

ABOVE THE DOOR that led outside, hung a camera, pointing right down the stairs.

"Oh no…" I said, frozen in place on the stairs while Courtney was already outside.

She turned around. "Oh, no? What now?"

I pointed at the camera in the corner. My hand was shaking from adrenaline and fear. "That. Did you see that before?"

She joined me back on the steps and looked up. "Crap. No, I didn't!" She gasped and her face went pale.

"What do we do now?" I asked, my mind racing, wondering if the camera was even functioning.

"We should smash it," I said. It seemed like the only immediate solution. Getting rid of the camera would remove any footage. No one would ever know we were there that night.

Courtney shook her head. "No, my parents have cameras, and if this is like those, it won't matter if we smash it. The recording is probably on an app on someone's phone or computer."

"So, they've already been seen then." It was a statement more than a question. The hope I had felt diminished. *Just when I thought things couldn't get worse.*

"I don't know," Courtney said, her face was ghost white.

I started walking away. We couldn't stay there, that was one thing I think we both knew. Courtney was at my side. "We didn't do anything wrong; we should just report this," I said. "If that camera is working and recording, it'll show that we walked in the same way we walked out. No blood on us, no weapons, and that the body was down there before our arrival and that we didn't bring the body in. But it would show who did."

"We were trespassing, Neve. That's a big deal." Courtney let out a long exhale. "We were trespassing on a crime scene."

"We're kids, we explore. I'd rather go down for trespassing than murder. And we're safer if the cops catch the killer. Especially if that camera is working."

We both knew that was true. Silently, between the two of us, the decision had been made. We would go back to Courtney's house to tell her parents and then the police.

CHAPTER SIX

AS WE NEARED HER HOUSE, both our phones pinged, alerting us that we'd both received a notification. As we approached the house, we pulled out our phones and checked the notification.

It wasn't a notification; it was a text message sent to the two of us. The words stopped us both in our tracks.

"No one will know what you saw, or you'll be the next victims to be discovered in the basement," I read aloud.

"Yeah, I got that too," Courtney confirmed. "Let's go fast." And we took off running towards her house.

Inside, her house was just a normal night. The TV blared from the living room and clanging came from the kitchen as her mom was probably cleaning and putting dishes away. No one noticed that we came in and headed up to Courtney's bedroom.

"What is going on?" Courtney asked, closing the door behind us and collapsing onto her bed. "Someone definitely saw us," she continued.

"And they know us," I said.

"Why would you say that?" Courtney asked. Sitting up, she looked at me as I sat on her floor.

"They texted us," I answered, "How else would anyone have our number?"

"Who do we know that would commit murder?" Courtney asked.

We sat in silence for a few moments pondering that question. Who did we know who could've killed someone? And if it wasn't someone we knew personally, who had our numbers and knew what our plans were?

"I still think we should report this," I finally said. "What could this person actually do once the police are involved?"

"I guess," Courtney replied. "Alright, yeah, let's talk and get it over with."

She stood up and slowly made her way to the door. As she placed her hand on the doorknob, both our phones pinged again. We looked at each other. *Was this a coincidence?*

Grabbing my phone, it was another anonymous text. I read it out loud as Courtney opened the message on her phone as well.

"If I go down, we go down together," the message read.

"What does that mean?" Courtney asked, returning to her bed to sit down.

For the third time that night, our phones pinged, alerting us of another anonymous message.

"I know what you did to Alexis." This time Courtney read the message out loud.

The message referred to the incident last year.

Courtney and Alexis were both in track with a big race coming up, and the prize was five thousand dollars. Courtney and Alexis competed against each other for who was the best, but Alexis was slightly better, physically. Courtney needed the money since her dad was out of work and her mom was having a rough time finding work.

Courtney couldn't lose that race, especially not to Alexis. Secretly, I had helped make sure Alexis couldn't run in that race, causing the win to go to Courtney. I'd waited for the right moment and pretended like I didn't see Alexis walking down the stairs in front of me and *accidentally* bumped into her. Alexis ended up breaking her collarbone and her ankle which meant she wasn't able to participate in the race and ultimately, Courtney won.

All eyes had been on her during that track meet. After the meet, she became the star of the team. The praise for her was high and her record was impeccable. She became unbeatable. There was little doubt that she would indeed be getting scouted.

If anyone ever found out about us setting up Alexis' injury, Courtney would lose her spot on the team. And she was depending on this team to get her an athletic scholarship for college. I would get in trouble too; expulsion would inevitably be the verdict, and I couldn't have that on my record.

"We can't say anything," I concluded.

How could we have said anything? Too much was on the line for us. Our futures could be ruined. This could also ruin our families and our reputations.

"What do we do now?" Courtney asked. She sat straighter, looking more serious.

I looked down at my phone and saw how late it had gotten. "I have to go home," I told her.

I stood up. "We don't talk about this," I said. My voice sounded more authoritative than I had ever heard myself sound before.

"Definitely not," Courtney agreed.

CHAPTER SEVEN

I LEFT her house the way I entered, through the front door. Just as when we had entered, no one acknowledged my passing through. Courtney's family was wrapped up in what they were doing. Or maybe they just didn't care who came and went through their house.

It was dark and chilly outside. Walking by myself, it felt darker and chillier than normal. I walked the few short blocks quickly, rushing faster than normal because the hairs on the back of my neck and arms stood straight up from the goosebumps.

Maybe I was being paranoid from the events of the night. Or maybe, just maybe, the feeling of being watched as I walked wasn't just a feeling, but something more.

I turned my head to peek behind me, but there was nobody there. I couldn't shake the feeling of someone's eyes boring into my back which justified those goosebumps.

I quickened my pace, almost at a full sprint now, towards my front door. As I reached for the doorknob and twisted, I realized that the door was locked. I grabbed my keyring out of my back pocket, which only housed two keys; our house key and the family car key. Although I wasn't yet old enough to drive, I kept the spare for the car just in case, you never know when this may be needed.

While attempting to unlock the door, the knob twisted and the door swung open. Jumping back, my heart pounded in my chest, and my mother stood before me.

"I thought I heard someone out here." She smiled at me, her brown eyes bright and calm.

"Geez, give me a heart attack, why don't you," I said, sarcastically.

CHAPTER EIGHT

MOVING OUT OF THE WAY, she stepped aside and let me join her inside.

"Jeremy is in the living room; we were just getting ready to call you," she stated.

With a confused look on my face, I asked, "Why did Jeremy come over?"

Jeremy was a friend of mine and Courtney's, but he was much closer to me than her, and I secretly wished he was more than just a friend. We spent a lot of time together, studying, talking about his girlfriends, or the boys I liked. I knew that he only saw me as a friend, but a girl can dream right?

"Homework?" My mom guessed, answering my question.

We smiled at each other knowingly before I walked into the living room to greet Jeremy.

Jeremy and I had been helping each other with school work for years now, even before high school started, usually with book reports, spelling words, and anything to do with reading and books. He was not a fan of books. Since Jeremy was strong in math, he would work with me throughout any of my struggles. Although, that year I was doing well in math without needing much of his help.

"Hey," I said when I walked into the living room.

"There she is." He laughed as he looked up at me from the couch. He was watching some Stars Wars show, eating straight from a bag of Doritos.

"What's up?" I asked, as I plopped down next to him.

"Bored," he replied.

I looked him in the eyes and raised an eyebrow questioningly at him.

"And I have a paper," he stated.

"Uh huh," I smiled. "That's what I thought. You could have messaged me instead of just coming here and waiting." I laughed.

"But, I always just come over," he responded, shoving more Doritos in his mouth.

That was true. Over the years, my home had become his second home. As far as my mom was concerned, he was family.

"Okay, I'll help." I rolled my eyes. "I have no choice." I laughed.

"But first let me finish this episode," he whined, "Please..."

"Fine," I groaned.

And we sat there together, watching the remainder of his show. For a second I forgot everything else that had happened earlier, probably because I felt safe within my home and with Jeremy. But that second was so brief because as soon as we both were silent for the episode, my mind went into overdrive, reminding me of everything that had occurred.

Who was texting us? Who was there in the woods with us? Who was on the other end of that camera that we saw at the top of the stairs leading to that basement?

Those were the questions playing on a loop in my head, over and over again, causing my anxiety to rise. I couldn't imagine knowing someone who was capable of murder. The feelings of assuming it had to be someone we knew had my heart racing within my chest. Those goosebumps I felt on my walk home had to mean something, right? The constant feeling of someone watching, listening, knowing everything that was going on with Courtney and me, it was nerve racking.

Those questions in my head must've consumed me, put me into a sort of trance and stolen the ability to be in the moment with Jeremy because I didn't snap out of it until I heard him talking directly to me.

"Hey, whatcha thinking about? I can see those wheels turning."

I looked over at him, his big, bright blue eyes were worried looking back at me. "Oh, nothing," I replied. "It's just been a long night."

"You mad at Courtney again?" He asked.

He was the one I talked to the most about Courtney, after all, he was basically my other best friend. Honestly, I was mad at her quite often. She was my best girl friend, but she could be the snottiest, rudest, most hurtful person, too. She was the type of person who thought she was joking when she would act or speak the way she did, and I did a good job at laughing along with her meanness, but she would hurt my feelings. Her words would cut like knives sometimes. That was probably why Jeremy distanced himself from her and also stopped hanging around her. Since Jeremy had also fallen victim to the things she had said, it became so easy for me to open up and talk about her with him. He understood where I was coming from and was there to support me.

"You could say that," I answered.

"Want to talk about it?" he asked.

"No," I answered. "Not right now."

He furrowed his eyebrows at me. He was probably confused because I never passed up a chance to talk about Courtney after she had pissed me off. "Okay," he finally said. He reached over the arm of the couch and pulled his book bag off the ground and into his lap. "Then let's take your mind off it by writing my paper."

I rolled my eyes at his statement, *my paper*. *He sure knew how to get my mind off of things*, I thought, laughing to myself.

He handed me the assignment directions to go over. Glancing over the sheet, he had to write a two thousand word essay on a book they had just finished reading in his English class.

"Did you take any notes?" I asked.

He responded by handing me his green spiral notebook with *English* sprawled across the front in black sharpie marker.

"Alright," I responded as I took that notebook from him and began rifling through the pages filled with his messy handwriting. While flipping the pages, my phone pinged with a notification. My heart dropped into my stomach. *Was it the killer again?*

CHAPTER NINE

GRABBING MY PHONE, I saw that there was another text message from the unknown number. The text read, *'Make sure your lips stay sealed.'*

Shock ran through my body, causing me to drop my phone onto the ground. My phone made a sudden thud in our quiet space, causing Jeremy to glance over at me with a puzzled look on his face.

"What the heck, Neve? You scared me! Who was that from?" He asked me, putting his phone down onto the table since he was scrolling through Instagram while I was browsing through his notebook.

"Uh, oh nothing," I stammered, trying my best to remain composed. "It was no one."

"Come on," Jeremy pressed. "I know you. I know you're upset. And you wouldn't have just dropped your phone like that if it was nothing."

Reaching down to pick my phone up off the ground, I kept my gaze down because I couldn't look him in the eyes. Jeremy had always had a way of knowing when something was wrong or off with me, and I knew if I looked directly at him, he would see right through me, knowing there was a problem. *A really big problem.* And that I was scared, scared for myself and Courtney, him, and of the unknown sender. I couldn't drag him into this.

"Was it Courtney?" he asked. "What are you girls fighting about this time?"

"It's really no big deal." I tried my best to sound casual, unaffected. I answered him while keeping my gaze down, because I could make myself sound confident, but my face would tell a different story, and I knew he would distinguish between those if I looked at him.

"But it is a big deal, Neve," he said. He stood up and put his hand out for me to take so he could pull me up off the couch. "Come on, let's go for a walk."

Even him mentioning the word walk brought me back to my walk home, and the feeling of someone watching or following me clouded my mind. "No," I said, ignoring his hand. "I'd rather stay in."

"Okay," he said, looking around the house. "Then let's go to your room and talk, at least tell me what happened tonight with Courtney."

So we went to my room, and behind us my mom called out, "Door open."

She knew we were just friends, but keeping doors open was a household rule. Plus, it was good to be able to see if anyone was poking around the halls and trying to listen at the door, because I didn't want anyone else to hear what I was going to tell Jeremy.

Knowing that Jeremy was trustworthy, I figured it would be okay to tell him about what we saw and about the messages Courtney and I were receiving. He already sensed that something was up, so I knew I would have to tell him anyway. No one else would know he knew anyway, right?

Guiding us both to sit on my bed, I spilled the entire story to him. How we were bored and wanted to go on an adventure. The abandoned house out in the woods behind the park. The one unlocked door that led us into the basement, the smell, the dead body, and the camera. There was so much to tell, but it felt good to be able to share this with someone else.

"And we've both gotten these messages from an unknown number, warning us not to say anything to anyone," I concluded my account of that night.

He sat there, staring at the floor. I sat crossed legged across from him, watching him, not knowing what was going through his mind. I wondered what he was thinking.

Did he think it was made up? Or did he think we were in real trouble and should still go to the police despite the unknown texter's warnings and threats? Although, I'd left out the threat that involved what happened to Alexis since I had never told him that story. I didn't want him to know what I did to help Courtney. I knew he'd say it was dumb to go that far to risk everything for myself and to help a friend who had been routinely cruel to me. I still didn't fully understand that myself, especially now that the memory had been brought back up. I was too ashamed of myself to confess any of it to him.

Finally, he looked up at me and said, "Damn. There's a house out behind Kitney Park?"

"That's what shocks you?" I asked, surprised, and

amused. "After everything else I already told you, your focus is on the abandoned house?"

"Well, I mean, who would've thought," he said, "You'd think it would've been discovered by now."

"We went farther in the woods than I've ever been," I explained. "Maybe no one ever wanted to travel that far either."

"Well, I want to go see it," he said.

"You can't," I said quickly.

"Why not?" he asked.

"Did you hear anything else I said?" I asked, a little angrier than I would've liked to be.

"Right," he answered, lowering his voice. "Dead bodies and killers."

I nodded. "I don't know what to do. But what we are wondering now is, who do we know who could do this?"

"What do you mean?" he asked. "Why would you think it's someone we know?"

"It would have to be someone we know. Whoever this is knows our numbers." I wanted to add, *and they know other things we've done.* But again, I didn't want to go into the Alexis story right now.

"Right," he responded. "This is crazy! And you guys really aren't going to say anything to anyone?"

"Well, except you," I said. "Please don't repeat this to anyone, not even Courtney. I really don't want her to know I told you."

"You have my word," he said, holding up his right hand giving me the scouts honor sign. "But I should be heading home now." He stood up, making his way towards my bedroom door.

"Wait," I said. "What about your paper?"

"I think you've got enough to deal with without helping me do my homework. I'll figure it out." He pushed my door, so it was completely open. "If anything else happens, call me right away. Okay?"

"Yeah." I shook my head. "But be careful walking home. On my way back here, I kind of felt like I was being watched or followed."

"Got it," he said. "I think you might've been a little paranoid though. I mean, I would've been, too."

"Maybe, but better safe than sorry Jeremy." I smiled. "Talk to you later."

Then he left. I heard him saying goodbye to my mom before I closed my door.

I laid on my bed, trying to calm my mind of the millions of thoughts and images that had been racing through it. *I really hope he makes it home safe.*

CHAPTER TEN

I MUST'VE FALLEN ASLEEP, because when I opened my eyes, my room was brightened by sunlight and early morning birds chirping outside my window. When I glanced around my room, I noticed my mom standing in my doorway. I gasped, wondering how long she had been standing there. *Was she watching me sleep?*

Sitting up and rubbing the sleep out of my eyes, I gazed at my mom quizzically, concerned about the worried expression on her face. *This is not exactly how I thought my morning would start.*

Finally, she looked at me and asked, "Did Jeremy say he was going anywhere before heading home last night?"

My heart sank into my stomach at the question. *Why was she asking me about Jeremy? Oh my God, did something happen to him?*

"No, why?" I asked.

"His mom just called me; she's been trying to get ahold of him because he didn't come home last night," she answered.

"He said he was going home," I replied, my voice shaky as my memory reminded me of how it felt as I walked home alone last night from Courtney's house. "He had a paper to work on."

"I'll have to let Mariann know," my mom said as she turned to leave my doorway. Mariann was Jeremy's mom. Our moms had only become friends due to Jeremy and I being so close our entire childhood. Otherwise, I don't think they would've ever met or built any type of friendship. They both had different interests, and very different lives. My mother was more on the athletic side, working as a trainer at the local gym. Jeremy's mom was artsy, working freelance jobs from home.

While rubbing the remainder of sleep out of my eyes, I reached for my phone, noticing it hadn't been where I placed it. It must have fallen to the floor while I was sleeping.

Unlocking my phone quickly to see if I had any missed calls or texts from Jeremy, I noticed that I had about twenty other notifications. Missed calls and texts, but nothing from Jeremy.

I really hope everything is okay with him!

Most of the texts were from Courtney, but I ignored hers because I was instantly pulled into the message from our unknown sender.

You opened your mouth when I told you not to. Now Jeremy suffers.

Courtney must've gotten the same message because her texts followed.

I didn't say anything!

We agreed to tell no one!

Why did you talk about it?!

Who else knows, Neve?!?!?!?!

ANSWER YOUR PHONE OR I'M COMING OVER!!

That was the last message she had sent, along with a bunch of missed calls, but I didn't bother calling her back. Based off her last text, she was probably on her way here anyway. *What would I have even said if I did call her back?*

Since I assumed that Courtney should be here any moment, I sent Jeremy a text. *Hey where are you? Your mom is worried.*

Not only was his mom worried, but I was too. I checked his social media accounts to see if he had been on any of them, but they showed he hadn't been active for nine hours. *Oh my God! That is since he left my house!*

That was so unlike him, he was always scrolling through Instagram. Now my worry about what was going on with him was really creeping up on me.

After all of this worrying, I knew that I needed to get a move on with my day. When I climbed into bed last night, I had fallen asleep in the same clothes I was in all day yesterday. I needed to get a shower in, wash this day-old makeup off my face, and change clothes before figuring out what my day ahead looked like.

Shutting my bathroom door and turning on the shower, I planned to get it all hot and steamy in here while I stripped down. The water temperature was perfect, hot as can be, just as I liked it. As much as I wanted to stay within the walls of this bathroom and thoroughly enjoy this shower, I knew that I had to make this quick because I had to figure out where Jeremy was.

Just as I was about to step out, the door swung wide open, hitting the wall. Standing in front of me was a very angry looking Courtney. *I guess she was telling the truth when she said she would come over if I didn't answer her.*

"Why haven't you called me back? Did you tell Jeremy, Neve?"

I reached out through the shower curtain to grab my towel so I could step out without standing in front of Courtney naked. "I kind of had no choice. He knew something was up," I replied while making my way over to the sink and mirror to brush my hair. "But none of that matters now. The most important thing now is that we find him."

"Find him?" Courtney questioned. "You mean he's not at home? Is that what that text means by *'Now Jeremy suffers'?*"

"Yes. His mom called my mom this morning wondering if he was still here. He walked home last night, but never actually made it home."

Heading out of the bathroom and to my bedroom, Courtney followed behind me, closing the doors behind us. Dropping the towel, I began to put on fresh clean clothes. *Wow! Even though that shower was quick and interrupted, I feel so much better!*

Courtney, who had been staring at her phone since she entered my room said, "And he hasn't been online since last night."

"That's why I'm even more worried. And he never texted me back either this morning," I said. "We have to find him, Courtney!"

"He didn't get back to me either," Courtney stated. "But that's not that weird, he rarely ever does any more."

"Like I said, let's just focus on trying to find him. As soon as I am finished getting dressed, we will come up with a plan," I said, not wanting to make this all about Courtney by rehashing the reasons why she thinks they don't talk that much anymore.

"What if we can't?" Courtney had said the one phrase that I had refused to let cross my mind until it had come out of her mouth.

"We will find him, Court, I know we will," I replied because I couldn't believe that something bad had actually happened to him.

CHAPTER ELEVEN

WE WALKED to the kitchen after I finished getting ready. My mom sat at the table, drinking coffee when we entered. She still looked worried, even while staring down at her phone. She looked up at us and said, "Jeremy's mom called the police."

Courtney gasped from behind me. "He really never came home?"

"He didn't," she replied, taking another sip of her coffee. "They may have some questions for you girls too, so be prepared for that. They usually question friends. Especially you, Neve, since he was here last." She looked deep in thought. "I feel responsible. I should have offered to drive him home."

"Mom, you can't blame yourself," I said. "He's been walking home from here since forever. He lives close by. Nothing has ever happened. You could never have known this would happen."

"I know. But still…" She trailed off, still looking really upset and defeated.

"We were actually going out to look for him," I told her.

"Let me drive you girls around," my mom offered.

"No, mom, it's okay," I said. "We won't go very far, just check a few places he hangs out at. And I have my phone." I tried my best to sound reassuring.

"I want you girls to stick together. And check in with me," she said. "I don't have work today, so I'll be home all day."

"Okay, Mom, we will, I promise," I replied. I made my way over to the counter to pour myself a cup of coffee to-go and asked Courtney if she would like one, too. With both of us having our coffee cups ready to go, we started to head towards the front door.

"You girls should eat something before you head out," my mom said. I hadn't even thought of eating. My stomach felt knotted, but I knew Mom was right. We needed to fuel up before embarking on this journey of finding Jeremy. I grabbed both of us some granola bars from the pantry, and tossed them into my purse. We probably wouldn't eat them, if I was being honest, but at least it was there in case we changed our mind.

Once we made it outside, I started walking in the direction of Jeremy's house. It wasn't far from my house, just about three blocks. I thought that maybe if I retraced his steps from my house to his, I would find clues that would tell us where he was. I'm not sure what kind of clues we would find, but it was worth a shot.

We found nothing.

Standing on the sidewalk in front of his house, I pulled out my phone to see if by some chance, maybe he had texted me back, but nothing was there. I had even checked his social media again. No activity, still. *What the hell, Jeremy? Where are you?*

My stomach sank deeper than I ever thought it could.

"Should we go in and see if maybe he came home before we got here?" Courtney asked, looking at Jeremy's front door.

I really didn't want to knock on his door and see his mom or the hurt she must be feeling. It would gut me even more. Somewhere deep down, I knew that he wasn't going to be there, though, especially since his mom told my mom that he never came home. I also knew if I saw her, I didn't want to lie to her about why Jeremy wasn't home. Or that I had told him a secret last night that put him in danger. *This was all my fault. I am so sorry, Jeremy!*

What if he had been home this entire time and his mom just didn't look everywhere? Maybe he fell asleep last night in the den, in front of the TV.

"Yeah," I answered. "Might as well cover all the bases."

CHAPTER TWELVE

BEFORE I COULD EVEN KNOCK on the door, a police car drove up and parked at the curb in front of Jeremy's house.

"What do we do?" Courtney asked quietly while nudging me.

"I don't know?" I said. I knew for sure it would look suspicious if we walked away right now, and I also knew that we couldn't say anything to the police right away either. I learned the hard way that saying things to the wrong people wasn't in our best interest and it was the reason Jeremy went missing. We couldn't risk hurting anyone else.

"We do what we came here for," I said quietly and knocked on the front door. "But we say nothing about last night to them," I finished.

Mariann opened the door just as two male officers approached her porch. She looked stunned to see us and the police.

"Did Jeremy ever come home?" I asked quietly.

"No, girls," she said, tears welling up in her already swollen eyes. She must've been bawling over Jeremy all morning, making my heart sink even deeper.

"Good morning, Mrs. Forester." One officer greeted her solemnly. "You are Jeremy Forester's mother, correct?"

"Yes." Mariann nodded. "I am."

"May we come in?" the same officer asked. "We just have a few questions."

"Please come in," Mariann said, stepping out of the way.

The officers walked in and the door shut behind them, leaving us outside, alone again.

We stood there for a few moments staring blankly at one another, unsure of our next move.

Jeremy hadn't returned and we didn't know where else to look for him. *Where could he possibly be?*

Then, it struck me. I didn't want to say it, but I knew it was a humongous possibility.

"We have to go back to the house," I finally said.

"What, your house?" Courtney asked. "Why?"

"No, not my house," I replied. "The house behind Kitney Park, in the woods."

"No way," Courtney said. "We can't!"

"Look, Jeremy was amazed that there was an abandoned house out there. After I told him what we found, his first response was that he wanted to go check it out," I explained. "What if he made a pit stop before going home? What if he's still there?"

Looking at Courtney, she looked apprehensive. I understood because her face looked how my stomach felt. Neither of us wanted to go back to that house or into that basement again. But if there was a chance Jeremy could have gone there last night and could possibly still be there, then we needed to know.

"Let's check," I stated. "We have to, and we'll be super quick about it."

We both looked at each other, knowing that we were both apprehensive, but we started off back to the old, abandoned house anyway. We walked there mostly in silence; the anxiety and dread we both felt was palpable.

My stomach rumbled, but not from hunger. It was from nervousness, lack of food, and probably the coffee we both drank this morning.

The walk seemed to take longer than I remember it being the first time, but that had to be because we were both so nervous about heading back there. We got lost one time, but we stopped when we finally saw the house. It looked even worse in the daylight. The roof was rotting, the porch had sunken in spots, and in general, the whole house just looked shambled and horribly old. *How the hell is this building still standing?*

From the outside there was no evidence of Jeremy. "We have to go inside to check, Courtney," I said.

Courtney groaned, "I really don't like this idea. Maybe we should go tell the police. They can check."

"We really can't," I said quickly. "Opening my mouth to Jeremy caused him to disappear. I can't put anyone else in danger."

Turning away from her, I headed towards the basement door. Upon glancing down, I stopped dead in my tracks.

CHAPTER THIRTEEN

THE DOOR STOOD WIDE OPEN, and track marks trailed from the top of the stairs like something had been dragged from the basement into the trees.

Courtney noticed the marks too, then said, "What the hell is that?"

Heart racing, I followed the drag marks to the tree line, only to notice that they continued beyond the trees and deeper into the woods.

"Do we keep following it?" Courtney asked.

"I really don't want to," I replied. My heart raced so fast I heard it thumping in my ears.

We both just stood there, looking at each other while glancing down at the path leading into the woods. The path went on far beyond our eyesight. Looking back at Courtney, I'm sure we had both had the same thoughts, *Was the body from the basement drug out? Or was it Jeremy's body?*

"Let's check the basement. Something was pulled from

down there. What if it was the girl's body we saw last night?"

Turning back towards the basement door, I felt Courtney silently creeping up behind me. Once we were back at the door, we paused briefly. *What if someone is still down there?* But after seeing those marks on the ground, I knew I had to head down there to see what was going on. *I really hope whoever is behind this isn't down there still!*

The outside light was only providing a dim light, so I pulled out my phone and turned on the flashlight, aiming it down the stairs.

There were muddied footprints along the steps that were now smeared and, it seemed, a little bloody.

After witnessing those footprints, we knew that we wanted to get in and out as fast as possible, so I quickened my pace.

Since the basement light was still off, I decided that it would be a good idea to leave it be and not turn it on. With the light from my phone and the sunlight coming in from the two small, dirt-caked, windows, we were able to see enough of the basement and what we came here for.

The basement looked the same, except the blood and dirt smeared path that led to the stairs.

We walked to where the body was propped up previously and Courtney gasped beside me. My thoughts were right, the body was gone. *I guess this wasn't Jeremy's body then, thank goodness!*

"Alright, time to get out of here!" I said and we ran out of the basement, up the stairs and back to the edge of the tree line where the path seemed to go on forever.

Looking at Courtney, hands on my hips, I said, "I have to know where this path leads."

"To a grave," Courtney said sharply. "Whoever did this, knows, obviously, and they buried the body. And they'll probably be back to cover up this path." She grabbed my arm and tugged me away from where we were standing. "We need to get out of here, now!"

My mind battled between my desperation to leave and my urge to follow the path until I finally decided against following the path. *What if the killer was still out there?* I had no desire to be the next victim. I already knew too much.

We both took off running until we were at Kitney Park, walking towards the swings. I needed to sit down, the anxiety and nervousness I was feeling was beginning to catch up with me and my legs felt wobbly.

My phone dinged, *probably another text message.* I pulled my phone out of my pocket as I sat down on the swing besides Courtney. Rocking up and down on the swing, I saw that it was a message from my mom. She was wondering where we were. I let her know that we were at the park and would be home soon.

Courtney looked at me questioningly, so I said, "It was just my mom wondering about where we were."

"Oh, okay," Courtney replied.

We sat there, gently swinging on the swings. Neither of us knew what to do at this point. If Jeremy had been at the abandoned house, it wasn't evident. The body that was there was no longer in the basement, so it must have been what was drug into the woods and was probably being buried as we sat there.

I still had the strongest urge to go back, follow the path and make sure that Jeremy wasn't there as well. If he was still alive and I could save him, I wanted to. The murderer took Jeremy. That was as much as we knew. But where was he? Was he still alive?

CHAPTER FOURTEEN

I FINALLY BROKE the silence by saying, "What if Jeremy is out there too?"

"I don't know, Neve. I just know I don't want to go back and get killed too," Courtney said, staring at her feet. "I just want to forget all this. I mean God, it's Saturday. We should be out having fun, not worrying about our lives ending abruptly."

Courtney's last statement triggered anger inside me. Of course, Courtney would be so selfish as to think that we should be doing something better. Something other than the right thing. "We can't forget this," I said intensely. "Jeremy is still missing! It's our fault. We need to find him. He might need our help."

"This isn't *our* fault. It's yours," she said rudely, "I kept my mouth shut like the text messages said. *You* didn't follow the rules. You're the reason Jeremy is missing."

Oh, of course, she blames me for all of it. Can't have little miss getting looked at in a negative light.

"If I didn't let you convince me to go out exploring in

the woods, we never would have been mixed up in any of this," I spat out while standing up.

"Where are you going?" Courtney asked.

"I'm going back," I said. "I need to know if Jeremy is out there."

"Neve, stop!" Courtney called from behind me, but I ignored her and continued walking as fast as I could down the path that would lead me to the abandoned house.

Courtney didn't have to come with me. I honestly didn't care either way. All I could think about was Jeremy. I needed to know for sure whether he was out there or not and if the killer had taken him too. Was this killer planning on killing him just as he killed the girl we saw in that wretched basement? *Please be alive, Jeremy!*

My mind ran on overdrive, thinking of all the horrible things that could be happening to Jeremy. My blood pulsed in my ears so loudly. When I made it back to the path near the abandoned house, I was shocked that Courtney was standing beside me.

I thought she was too scared and selfish to follow me back out here. But there she was; I guess people can surprise you sometimes.

I took a step onto the path, but Courtney's hand gripping tightly to my arm stopped me from continuing.

"I really think you won't like what you see when you get out there," she said softly, nervously. "Neither of us will," she quickly added.

"I need to know," I stated, pulling my arm back from her grip. "You can stay, but I won't. I need to make sure Jeremy isn't out there or in any danger."

"It might be too late," Courtney said from behind me.

Why is she acting like this now?

I didn't even acknowledge her last statement. I just walked cautiously down the path that was laid out before me. As quickly as I wanted to make it to wherever this path ended, I knew I had to go slow. To be as quiet as possible. I didn't want to be found and become the killer's next victim. I watched every step I took, making sure not to step on any sticks, leaves, or anything that would make a sound.

My phone rang out loud, alerting me that I received a text message. Before checking the message, I turned down the volume, something I should've already done, though.

It was from an unknown number, again. It read, *'Keep Jeremy safe. Turn back now.'*

I stood there, frozen in place for a few moments, maybe even longer. The killer knew I was on his tail. *But how?* I turned around, debating whether I should turn back or not. I could hear footsteps behind me which kept me locked in place even more. Slowly, Courtney approached. *I can't believe she came after all.*

"I got another message, Neve," she said, timidly. "You need to come back. This isn't safe."

"I have to go," I heard myself say, although I knew in my mind I should probably listen to her. I just couldn't leave without knowing that Jeremy was okay.

"Okay then, I think I need to go with you," she said, and we started back down the path. We went as quickly, but quietly, as we could.

The more we walked, the faster my heart raced. I was scared, but somehow, I didn't turn around. I think the courage came from my desperation to see for myself that Jeremy was still alive.

As we approached the end of the trail, I grabbed ahold of Courtney's hand and led us around to hide behind some large trees, hoping it would keep us from being seen by the killer.

We could both hear labored breathing and what sounded like a shovel hitting dirt.

We peered around the trees, and what I saw made me gasp. Shock slowly began to take over my body.

CHAPTER FIFTEEN

JEREMY STOOD BEFORE US, throwing dirt in a pile and packing it down, digging a hole.

"Oh my God, he's okay," I whispered to Courtney. "It looks like the killer is making him bury the body. We have to get him out of here."

"Wait," Courtney said. But it was too late. I was already running toward Jeremy, calling his name as quietly as I could.

He saw me and stood straight. His whole body tensed up. He seemed so angry and irritated that I froze right there in my tracks, scared.

He threw the shovel violently to the ground. "What'd I say!" he shouted, looking behind me at Courtney. "You were supposed to keep her away from here!"

What is happening right now?

Courtney stepped out from behind the tree and shrugged. She seemed nervous. "I tried, hun. I sent her another text, but she didn't listen." *Courtney was the one texting me this whole time?*

I took a few steps back, looking back and forth between Courtney and Jeremy. I was so confused, and my thoughts raced, matching pace with my pounding heart. I wasn't thinking clearly. It never occurred to me that Jeremy could have potentially been the bad guy in this whole situation. *Nothing makes any sense!*

What were they talking about? Standing there, confused, I started piecing everything together in my mind. And like a lightbulb turning on inside my head, I knew what was happening.

"W-wait," I stammered. "You two?" I pointed to Jeremy, then Courtney. "You two did this? Worked together?" Things were slowly starting to dawn on me, things that I had never in a thousand years thought would ever occur.

They looked at each other, then at me.

"You weren't supposed to find out, Neve," Jeremy said in a forced sweet voice.

"But why?" I asked. It was the only thing I could think to say as I was trying to figure out the reasons they may have had. That had always been who I was, the girl who would give everyone the benefit of the doubt. Just as I was doing right then.

I watched as Jeremy walked over to Courtney and threw an arm around her waist. She looked up and kissed him on the cheek before saying, "This was mostly my idea, but Jeremy helped. Didn't you, hun?"

Why does she keep calling him hun? What was her idea? Though things were slowly starting to dawn on me, not everything was making complete sense in my confused state of mind.

"Well, you know, I saw Courtney by the girl, and knew

she wouldn't be able to get rid of the body herself." Jeremy looked down on Courtney lovingly. It hit me then that they were together, and had probably been sneaking around behind my back this whole time.

"How long?" I asked.

"How long, what?" Jeremy said, still looking at Courtney.

"How long have you two been together? Sneaking around?" I spat. Anger rose in my chest, dulling out every other emotion I had been feeling. Of course, Courtney got him first, she knew I liked him, so she just had to get him before I could even have a chance. Just like always, she had always needed to one up me.

"Since last summer," Courtney said slyly, looking from Jeremy to me.

The school year before last summer was when Jeremy stopped hanging out with Courtney. It had taken me until that moment to realize that them getting together was probably the reason why. The whole time before that I had just thought that it was because he couldn't stand Courtney.

I looked at the pile of dirt that now had a dead girl's body beneath it and asked, "Who was the girl?" changing the subject before the anger and betrayal caused me to start crying.

They exchanged a worried glance, then Country said, "It was Amara."

Amara was friends with Alexis. And they weren't just casual friends either. They were best friends and had been since kindergarten. They were inseparable. Some people thought they were more than friends, despite them each having their own boyfriends.

"Amara saw what you did," Courtney continued. "She knew it wasn't just an accident, even though it may have looked like one. She spent months trying to figure out why you bumped Alexis down the stairs. When she finally realized it was so I could win, she confronted me.

"She said you were too nice to plan to hurt anyone. She knew I was behind Alexis being injured. She told me to turn myself in, but I couldn't do that. You'd get in trouble, too. We met up at Kitney Park, and I told her I wasn't going to say anything if she wasn't either. But, then she threatened to tell on me anyway. And she was actually going to, until I stopped her.

"See, I am a great friend to you. Now you won't get expelled," Courtney gloated as Jeremy wrapped his arm around her waist again.

"You are a great friend." He smiled and leaned down to kiss her, causing more anger and betrayal to rise into my chest. Tears flooded behind my eyelids, but I refused to let them flow. The last thing I wanted was those two seeing me cry.

"And good thing I was around," Jeremy continued. "I saw Court hit Amara in the head with that rock as she walked away. I was on my way back from that abandoned house when-"

"Wait, you already knew about the house?" I asked, astounded. "You acted totally surprised when I told you."

"My acting skills can be phenomenal," he said, releasing Courtney's waist to take a bow.

"Not a lot of people have been deep enough into the woods to discover it, but believe it or not, quite a few people do know and actually hang out there. That's why I buried the body. Some seniors are planning a party here next weekend."

"If you knew the body was there, why did you take me there?" I asked Courtney.

"Well, Jeremy didn't exactly tell me the body was there," Courtney explained. "I just had a hunch, and I wanted to make sure."

"Why bring me?" I asked.

"I didn't want to go alone. I wanted you there," Courtney answered, adding. "I thought it would be a good idea to have you with me, to make the whole exploring the woods story more believable. Just in case."

"In case what?" I nearly yelled. I was hurt, confused, and was beginning to become very angry at the fact that Courtney wrapped me up in this. I was being used as her alibi. I wished that we never went out there. I should have refused to go exploring with her.

I started to storm off. I wanted to go back home. Go back to sleep. Forget that any of this had ever happened.

"Where are you going?" Jeremy asked.

I spun around and said angrily, "Home."

Before I could turn around and start walking again Jeremy said, "Oh you can't go home."

"Why not?" I spat.

"We can't trust you not to turn us in," Courtney answered on behalf of Jeremy.

"You're angry," Jeremy said "About more than just this." He gestured at the area where he had just buried Amara. "I know you've had a thing for me for a long time now, and your reaction to me and Courtney... You're definitely angry about that too. You have so many reasons and motivations to turn us in."

"You have already said multiple times you wanted to tell our parents or the police," Courtney chipped in.

"So have you," I said to her.

"That was all part of the act," she explained.

"Well, you two can keep your act going together," I said, anger in my voice. "Just leave me out of this, I won't say anything to anyone."

With that, I turned and started walking away again. After two steps, a hand gripped tightly around my arm, stopping me in my tracks.

CHAPTER SIXTEEN

"YOU'RE part of this whether you want to be or not," said Jeremy, who still tightly gripped my arm, preventing me from running away like I wanted to.

"See, I really don't believe that if we just let you walk away, that you really won't say anything or turn us in," he continued. "I know you, remember? This will eat you up until you feel like you're going to explode and that need to tell someone will eat you alive. I mean, that's why you told me about *this* situation, right?"

"So, then what?" I asked. "Are we staying out here all night? You know your mom has the police already looking for you? They'll find us anyway."

There was a moment of silence as Jeremy and Courtney pondered what I had said. I looked from Courtney to Jeremy again thinking about how these two had been my best friends, but they betrayed me in so many ways, and now they sat there contemplating what to do with me. *What has my life become?*

I have to get as far away from them as I can. But before I could make a move, Jeremy looked at me and said, "We won't stay here, but you will. I have an idea."

"You always have the best ideas," Courtney complimented while bouncing on her feet, gazing at Jeremy with that same *loving* look she had in her eyes earlier.

Jeremy, still holding tightly onto my arm, led us along the path and back to the abandoned house.

We walked away, quickly and without anyone speaking a single word. Upon reaching the basement door of the house, he led me into the basement and straight to that same rusted water pipe that Amara had been tied to. I was horrified. *Is he going to leave me down here? Is he planning to kill me too?* I studied his face, watching how his eyes never drifted from me. I had never seen Jeremy as someone to fear until that moment.

Without taking his eyes off me, he said to Courtney, "There's some rope on the top shelf on the other side of the room. Bring it to me."

She did as Jeremy had said, grabbing the rope off of the shelf and bringing it right to Jeremy, with a big smile on her face. *Of course she did.* Once she handed him the rope, he tied my wrists behind me, circling it around the pipe, trapping me in that nasty, decay-smelling basement.

My heart pounded. *This isn't good. How will anyone find me down here?* Once they secured me to the pipe, I lowered myself so I sat on the ground and watched them look satisfied as they stared at me.

Jeremy walked towards the stairs with Courtney trailing right behind him. I felt a moment of relief when they turned away, leaving. *They weren't going to kill me.*

That brief thought diminished quickly when I realized that they were going to leave me here. Alone.

"Wait," I screamed louder than I meant to. They turned simultaneously, heads cocked, staring at me. "You can't just leave me down here. What are you going to tell the police? What about my parents?"

"You guys found me," Jeremy said. "Saved me from the killer. Courtney and I got away, you were too slow. The killer got you," He explained with a conniving smile.

You bastard!

Courtney laughed. "You should always stretch before trying to run away from a killer, Neve. I always tell you you're too slow because you never stretch." They both laughed at her stupid senseless joke like it was the funniest thing they had ever heard. "Or maybe it's just because you're too short. Too slow."

Always with the snide remarks, she never quits, does she?

They started to turn to leave, but I yelled again, "Wait. The party. Isn't there going to be a senior party here?" I was happy that in my panic I remembered a key detail in Jeremy's story from earlier.

"We'll get rid of you before then, don't you worry," Jeremy answered. Then he grabbed Courtney's hand to pull her up the stairs.

But before they both went up the stairs, Courtney said, "Wait," and walked over to me. She reached her hand into my back pocket and grabbed my phone, holding it up to show Jeremy. "We almost forgot! She can't be left down here with this, hun."

With my phone in her hand, she walked back over to Jeremy and he grabbed her around the waist while looking at me and said, "What would I do without you?"

Then that was it, they left, gone, leaving me all alone in this nasty, decaying basement. With the two of them gone, I could hear the beating of my heart thumping through my chest. *How am I going to survive this?*

CHAPTER SEVENTEEN

I KNEW I had to figure out how to free myself, to escape. I looked around the dimly lit basement. Anything that could possibly help me was too far away. Not that I could've grabbed anything anyway.

I twisted my wrists in circles behind my back. The rope he tied them together with was itchy and rough. I could already feel the rash on my wrists forming. But I ignored that pain. There was about a quarter-inch gap between my wrists to play around with. I took a few steps forward until my arms were as straight out behind me as I could get them. With my elbows locked in place, I positioned the gap as best as I could to the pipe and separated my wrist to put tension, hoping to widen the gap and pull free. I pulled my arms as hard as I could, feeling the rope eat into my flesh. I felt the warm, wetness of my own blood dripping down onto my wrists. This pain caused me to scream out, *how did I get myself into this position?*

After what felt like forever, my right arm finally broke free. I was sure the slipperiness of my blood helped speed up the process of getting out of the rope. After I examined both bloody wrists, I threw the rope on the ground.

I ran up the stairs, out the door, and through the woods faster than I had ever remembered myself running. *I had to stop them.* That had been my only motivation. They couldn't get away with this, any of this. It was all a lie. They definitely wouldn't be getting rid of me, either.

I caught up with them just before Kitney Park. They both spun around to face me as I approached. I could see that they had been whispering amongst themselves, probably making plans as to what to do with me. Their shocked expressions pleased me in a strange way. They underestimated me. They thought I was too weak to escape and too slow to catch up with them before they could return to Jeremy's house and feed the police and his mom their fake story.

I couldn't let their plan succeed.

I stopped in front of them with my hands on my knees trying to catch my breath. Running as fast as I had, had taken everything out of me. But nothing was speeding this process up, especially with the anger building back up within me.

"We should've just killed her," Courtney said, rolling her eyes.

"Well, well. Look who's faster than I thought," Jeremy said while looking towards me, making Courtney laugh, which made me even angrier.

How could she possibly be laughing right now?

I wasn't sure yet of what my exact plan would be, but I knew they weren't returning to Jeremy's house without me. I stepped back quickly as Jeremy stepped towards me, making an effort to grab me. My quick movement caused him to miss, making his raised hand fall back down to his side.

"Stop!" I shouted, loud enough to be heard by others, before either of them could say anything. I could hear people at the park just on the other side of a few thin trees before us. *This is my chance!*

"Quiet!" Courtney said, looking nervous. "I don't want anyone to hear you. It'll ruin the plan."

"It doesn't matter who hears me," I said loudly again, still a little out of breath. "And the plan is changing. I'm going with you. We both saved Jeremy today. The killer took off, I don't know." I was saying things as they popped into my head at that point.

"That doesn't sound believable," Courtney said in a mocking tone. "The killer just left without another victim? Like anyone will believe that, Neve."

"Three against one? Sounds kind of believable, actually," Jeremy said, looking between me and Courtney. "But you two don't look like you just fought off a killer. How can we fix that?"

It was hard to believe that the three of us were formulating a story to give to the police, to cover up Courtney's crime.

Why am I involving myself like this? I said I wanted to take them down.

But as my breath finally slowed down and I could think a little more clearly, my anger grew more intense, knowing that this was the only way that we could walk away from this without the two of them killing me. I stepped towards Courtney and punched her in the eye. The sound of my fist colliding with her face made me smile, despite the pain in my knuckles, I felt satisfied.

"There. Looks believable now. I've been wanting to do that for a long time." I smiled, because punching her truly did feel satisfying.

Courtney stood there holding her left eye. Swelling and redness began to form quickly. Jeremy looked shocked. "You're just full of surprises today," he said to me as he walked over to Courtney and held her face gently in his hands.

"You okay?" he asked.

"Yeah," she said in a defiant voice, stepping away from him and marching straight towards me. "Bitch," she yelled as she punched me in the mouth. She caught me by surprise, so I didn't get a chance to dodge her. The impact of her fist stunned me before the actual pain settled in.

Hot, searing pain soared across my face, and I could taste blood. Bringing my hand to my mouth, I could feel a split in my bottom lip, swollen and dripping with blood. I ran my tongue across all of my teeth to make sure I wasn't missing any.

Jeremy stood back, watching. He had a grim look across his face, both worried and amused. "Well, you both look like you've been in a fight. Should be much more believable now."

"Now we just need a really good story to stick to," I said, trying to think fast.

"Neve and I were bored yesterday, so we went out exploring last night and found the abandoned house. When we told Jeremy, he decided that he wanted to check it out by himself. But when he got there, the killer got to him first. Today, Jeremy was missing, and we just knew that it had something to do with that house. We headed back to that house and that's when we found Jeremy, along with the killer in the basement. The killer tried to grab us too, but we fought him off and the three of us took off running back home," Courtney said.

"But I guarantee the cops are going to ask us other questions, so we need to think and be on the same page with our story. Like, what did the killer look like?" Jeremy said.

"Uhh, well we don't know exactly. Definitely a man, tall. But his face was covered with a ski mask," Courtney explained.

"What if they want to search our phones?" I asked. "And they see the anonymous text messages you've been sending me?"

She reached into the back pockets of her jeans, she handed me my phone back. "Delete them. Then clean out the trash. I'll delete everything on my end including the app that made my number anonymous."

CHAPTER EIGHTEEN

WHEN WE WERE FINISHED DELETING everything and ready to run back to Jeremy's house, Jeremy looked at me skeptically and said, "I still don't trust that you won't crack."

"I won't," I said firmly, even though I knew I was bad at lying. But I had convinced myself of this story we came up with and believed that I could stick with it. "Why would I? We would all go down for this if I cracked, myself included. I don't want that. I just want to forget any of this happened."

"Fine. I guess we will go back to my house then," Jeremy said.

I could tell by his voice that he still wasn't fully convinced that he could trust me. I had no choice but to be trusted with this. The last thing I wanted was to get into trouble and face whatever consequences would come my way. Not only for the stuff that happened with Alexis, but also for being a part of this whole lie.

The three of us walked side-by-side through Kitney

Park. There were children playing, laughing and running, parents nearby chatting with each other as they watched their kids. It was a nice cool fall day. The kind of day where the three of us used to walk over to each other's houses or ride bikes to the corner store to get snacks. We used to be great friends, have lots of fun, but just like that, everything changed for the worse. I would never be able to think of either of them as my friend again. I wanted nothing to do with either of them, but now we were glued together by this huge lie. *I will never be able to trust them again, but I had to with this.* There was no other choice.

As we approached the intersection to Jeremy's house, he looked at me and Courtney, "You two got the story down, right? We can't afford to mess this up." He repeated the story of Courtney and I exploring because we were bored, coming back and telling him about the abandoned house and then going to explore it by himself. Then he would get kidnapped by a psychopathic killer until we came and rescued him. The killer then took off, never to be seen again.

To me the story just didn't seem to be very believable, but I found myself repeating after Courtney as she said, "Yes, got it." I must have sounded more positive than I felt because Jeremy then led the way all the way to his front door, where he twisted the knob and walked in.

His mom ran to us at the doorway and paused. She seemed shocked at first, then a flood of tears streamed from her eyes, down her cheeks, dripping off her chin as she ran towards Jeremy and wrapped him up in a hug. Courtney and I stood back and watched. My eyes filled with tears, not because of the emotional moment between

Jeremy and his mom, but because we were about to lie to her. *I hate this so much!*

"Where were you? What happened? Why are you dirty?" His mom was spitting out questions faster than Jeremy could even respond.

"It's a crazy story, Mom," he answered, turning his head to look at us. "But I'm okay now." He smiled reassuringly while pointing in our direction. "Thanks to these girls." You could see the relief leaving his mom's face as she reached out and hugged him again.

"Oh, I'm so happy," his mom said, letting him go and wiping her face. "I have to call the officers and let them know you came home. They've already started a search."

Courtney and I gave each other a worried glance. *Please let this go according to plan!* Jeremy's mom stepped into the kitchen to call the police, leaving the three of us standing in the entryway. We knew that we had to make this story believable, just as much as our mannerisms needed to be on point. Jeremy led us into his living room, where he collapsed onto the brown suede sofa with Courtney sinking down right beside him while I sat in an armchair across from them.

The events from last night played through my mind as I sat there. It was then that I remembered the camera. "Jeremy," I whispered.

He looked over at me.

"What about that camera? If we tell your mom about the abandoned house, the cops will go there and see the camera too. Can't they track it?"

"I already checked that out," Jeremy explained. "It's a wireless camera, but there are no batteries in it. There never were. Some seniors probably took them out when they started partying there so they wouldn't get caught doing things they shouldn't be doing anyway."

That slightly relieved me. It was, after all, one less thing to worry about.

The three of us just sat there silently until Jeremy's mom came into the room. "The police are on their way. They are going to have lots of questions, and probably some paperwork for us to fill out. But before they get here, please tell me what happened," she begged. Tears still streaming down her cheeks, she looked just as shaken up as she sounded. My heart broke for her, and a wave of guilt washed over me as I realized we were about to tell her a huge lie that only we knew about.

She's always been another mom to me, how can I possibly get through lying to her?

CHAPTER NINETEEN

THE THREE OF us looked at each other again. I was nervous and didn't want to be the first to speak. I think Courtney sensed my hesitation because she opened her mouth after glancing at me, "I feel like this is all my fault. I was bored last night while Neve and I were hanging out. We went exploring in the woods behind Kitney Park, and found an old, abandoned house out there."

She finished explaining how when we got back, I told Jeremy, and he was amazed and wanted to go explore it himself. "They didn't know I was going to go last night. I told Neve I was going home," Jeremy explained. "I just wanted to see it for a second, but when I got there, I wasn't alone. There was this man there. He was big and wearing a ski mask. I thought that was weird, since it wasn't that cold last night. The guy caught me as I was trying to sneak into the basement and ended up tying me up down there."

Jeremy looked down. He was doing a great job at looking sad and scared. Then he looked over at Courtney and said, "They found me. That guy was dragging me out into the woods. They attacked him. And then everything happened so fast. Once my hands were free, I started attacking that guy too. He ended up taking off. I think he got spooked, maybe heard someone else in the woods. But we ran straight here."

Jeremy's mom was sobbing, with her hand over her mouth, probably trying to stifle her crying. My heart broke watching her cry. She was probably feeling a bunch of different emotions, one of which was fear. She believes us, that there was someone out there who tried to take her son, and in her mind, that fake person is still out there. *How could we do this to her?*

When I looked over at Jeremy, I could feel him staring at me while I watched his mom break down. I knew that he was studying me, seeing if I was showing signs of buckling under the guilt. He'd always been able to sense my feelings. But even though our story was coming across as truthful, I couldn't help feeling guilty. I hated lying. Especially when the result was watching someone believe the lie and cry the way his mom was right in front of me.

I knew, though, that telling the truth now would ruin not just me, but Courtney and Jeremy too. So, I gave Jeremy a reassuring look. He looked at me quizzically, then looked back over at his mom who was still frantic about the entire situation.

There was then a knock on the door. We all knew it was the police returning to ask their questions. *Are they going to believe our story or will they see right through it?* My thoughts made my anxiety soar, while my heart felt like it was going to jump right out of my chest. Tears filled my eyes as Jeremy's mom went to let them in. *We can do this, we can do this!*

The next hour or so was spent talking with the police in a group setting, in the living room. But then the two police officers took Jeremy into the kitchen and me into the dining room. Leaving Courtney alone with Jeremy's mom.

It had been easier to speak with the police as a group, but alone, I felt more anxious. Tears rolled down my cheeks as I answered question after question, hoping the officer would see my tears as fear and relief that Jeremy was okay, rather than as my nervousness of having to lie.

As we went over the story again, confirming what was said as a group in the living room, it was hard to tell whether I was believable. The officer was stone-faced, emotionless. After he was done talking with me, he thanked me and led me back into the living room. Courtney was now in the kitchen talking with the officer who had previously been talking with Jeremy. Jeremy was now sitting beside his mom. Comforting her. She was no longer crying, but the worry remained plastered all over her face.

I stood up. I had to leave. I couldn't stand to see the expression that Jeremy's mom wore any longer, especially since I knew that I caused that look. I needed to go home. I remember feeling as if my bed was calling to me. It was my safe place, and I needed to be in it.

"Where are you going?" Jeremy asked in a demanding tone that I wasn't used to.

I looked at him, studying his face. This was not my Jeremy. My Jeremy was kind, loving. He was my friend who would never lie to me. The feeling of betrayal hit me again because everything I knew Jeremy to be, everything he was to me, vanished after that day. He was just an actor. A character he pretended to be around me. Behind my back, he was his real self, the one I no longer trusted. I no longer wanted to tell him my secrets or share my thoughts with him. I could no longer stand to look at him.

"Home," I answered. And before he could object, I was out the door, sprinting. I had never moved so quickly in my life.

CHAPTER TWENTY

WHEN I WALKED through the door of my home, my mom was there to greet me. She asked me what was going on and if we had found Jeremy. I told her most of the story that we had conjured.

"Yes, Jeremy was found, but he was kidnapped by a murderer, and the police questioned us while we were at his house. I'm sure they're out searching for the guy who tried to hurt Jeremy by now." I anticipated the police would be contacting her also.

I felt sick lying to my mom, but I knew I had to keep the story going. Only I felt that my motive had changed, and I wanted to protect myself. I hoped deep down that the police would see the lie and view me as ignorant to what had actually happened, and the lies Courtney and Jeremy had told. I wished that I could remain innocent in this whole thing once the real story started to unfold. *One can dream, right?*

I lay in my bed, letting the tears flow down my cheeks. At some point, I must have fallen asleep because I woke up to my phone ringing and the sun shining through my window in a different position than it was when I entered my room.

I grabbed my phone, seeing Courtney's name across the screen. I should have let it continue ringing, but I answered out of habit before my brain could convince me to ignore it.

"What?" I said, instead of, 'Hello?'. My voice was monotone, dry, and emotionless. I felt numb emotionally. I just wanted this nightmare to all disappear.

"You just left?" She was angry, but I didn't care. "You need to come over to Jeremy's. I'm still here and we all need to talk. Now!"

"Talk about what?" I asked, tonelessly.

"About.." She paused. "Well, just come over. It's better if we do all of our talking in person."

I remained silent for a long moment, and she asked, "Are you still there?"

"Yes, I'm still here. I'll try to be there soon," I said as I rolled my eyes. I didn't want to go, but knowing Court-ney, she wouldn't give up until I did. And part of me was also curious about what still needed to be talked about and what other lies they wanted me to tell to keep them safe.

As I was about to open the door, my mom came running up. "Where are you off to?" she asked.

I hesitated because of the worried look on her face. "Jeremy... needs company," I stammered. "I just think he's still freaked out and doesn't want to be alone."

"Do you really think it's safe to walk there alone? I can drive you," she said. "You know I know about what happened... what you kids have already been through. If there's still a psychopath out there trying to kidnap kids… It's just, it's not safe."

"Mom, I'll be fine," I said, giving her the best reassuring look I could muster up. "It's still daylight outside, and it's not a far walk. I'll text you as soon as I get there, okay?"

She still looked worried but agreed to let me go on my own. After she walked out of my room, I grabbed my phone and headed out, making my way quickly back over to Jeremy's house. I wanted to get there fast, talk fast, and get back home. I needed to get this day over with. If I could, I would never talk to either Jeremy or Courtney ever again. *Life couldn't be that easy though, right?*

As soon as I arrived at Jeremy's door, I texted my mom to let her know I got there safely. I didn't need her worrying anymore than she thought she needed to. After texting my mom, I knocked and Jeremy's mom answered and let me in. She told me Jeremy and Courtney were both in Jeremy's room, so that's where I headed. They were both sitting crossed legged on his bed. They had been whispering, but stopped to look at me as I came in.

"What?" I asked, crossing my arms over my chest. "What do we still need to talk about?"

"Close the door," Jeremy said, and I turned around and did as he asked.

"You know Amara has been missing for close to a week now," Jeremy whispered. "The police think the person who kidnapped me is the same person who took Amara. They suspect she is dead."

"Well, she is," I said, loudly.

"Shh," Courtney said with her index finger in front of

her lips. "Jeremy's mom has been hovering, and she can't hear any of this."

Jeremy quickly stood up and cracked the door to peek out, checking to see if his mom was out there listening. He closed the door again quietly and turned to us. "We're safe for now," he said as he sat back in the same place on his bed. "But we need to be careful, and quiet."

"Okay. So?" I whispered.

"They're going to go out looking around Old Kitney Park. What if they find her body?" he asked. "Our finger-prints are probably all over her."

"Maybe, maybe not," I spoke.

"Well should we, maybe get rid of her better?" Courntey asked. "Like put her somewhere else?"

"How are we going to do that?" I asked, still standing with my arms over my chest. "I say we just leave those woods behind Old Kitney alone. Let everything play out from here. Even if they do find Amara, how can they prove that it was you two?" I turned to the door. *I've had enough of this!* "I'm going back home; this whole thing has my mom so freaked out."

Before I could open the door, it swung open, almost hitting the left side of my body. Jeremys' mom came in, pressing the screen of her phone into her stomach. The expression she wore on her face shook me to the core.

CHAPTER TWENTY-ONE

"THEY FOUND a dead girl's body; they think it's that missing girl from your school they brought up earlier. Amara, I think, was her name. They want to know if you ever saw her body while the killer had you?" she asked Jeremy.

"No," Jeremy said quickly, too quickly.

I looked at Courtney who, I could tell, thought his quick response was suspicious as well.

His mom didn't catch on, she put her phone back up to her ear and left Jeremy's room. "He said no, he never saw her," we heard her say to whoever she was talking to. Probably one of the same officers who were here all day and questioned us.

I grabbed onto the doorknob of Jeremy's now open door. "Looks like it's too late to worry about that now," I said, turning to leave once again.

"Wait," Jeremy said.

"No, I'm going back home. I'm done with all of this for today," I said as I turned to leave.

I wanted to make sure I kept my mom in the loop on what was going on, so I texted her to let her know I was on my way back home. Making quick use of my feet, I walked down the street, heading right towards my house.

The very next morning, I woke up to a call from Jeremy. He asked me to meet him at Kitney Park. "Something happened last night that we all need to talk about," he said, sounding anxious.

"Why can't you just tell me now?" I asked, frustrated.

"It's not something we can just talk about on the phone. Our phones could be being monitored or something. Just come, and hurry up."

Putting on a plaid zip-up sweater, pulling my black boots over my jeans, and throwing my hair up quickly, not really caring what I looked like, I finished getting myself ready for what lay ahead today. My mom stopped me again as I tried to leave. She was worried about us all hanging out at the very park where Amara's body was found. *I don't blame you for being worried mom, you should be. This is breaking my heart.*

I convinced her that it was okay since we would be together, and I would call the police if anyone suspicious came around. It broke me seeing her so worried about an imaginary killer being on the loose. I wanted to tell her the truth so badly, but the truth was that I was going to talk to the actual killers, about the lies they wanted me to continue telling to keep them safe. I knew I couldn't very well tell her that. So instead, I just told her, "I'll be back soon. Very soon." Because that was the actual truth. I didn't want to spend any more time with Jeremy and Courtney than I had to.

I walked quickly to the park. When I arrived, Jeremy

and Courtney sat side by side on the swing. They looked upset, and I wondered what was wrong this time. Whatever it was, I was sure it wasn't my fault because all I did was go home, eat, and go to sleep last night.

Jeremy stood as I approached. When I was close enough, he held up his phone. There was a text message from an anonymous sender that read, *"I know what you did to Amara, and neither of you will get away with this."*

Courtney then held up her phone revealing that she had gotten the same exact message.

I was silent for a second, then it dawned on me that this was probably Courtney trying to scare us. "You never deleted that app huh?" I asked her suspiciously.

"What are you talking about?" she asked bewildered. "The app is gone; it has been since I told you I was deleting it. This isn't from me."

"Wait a minute though," Jeremy asked, eyeing her cautiously. "How do we know this wasn't you? The whole anonymous text idea was your idea."

"I've been with you this whole time; I slept over at your house. You would've known if it was me texting you," she said defensively.

"Well, we were together when I was getting the anonymous texts that were actually coming from you. So, are you doing this?" I asked.

"Just tell us," Jeremy said.

"It's not me!" Courtney shouted, frustrated that we wouldn't believe her.

"Ugh." I rolled my eyes. I was angry that they had me come out there to talk about another lie Courtney started. "I'm so sick of this." I turned and started walking away.

Courtney grabbed my arm. "It's not me. Here, check

my phone. The app is gone." She thrusted her phone into my chest.

I grabbed it instinctively to prevent it from falling to the ground. "You could've just deleted the app after you sent the message." I replied, giving her phone back to her.

"Just stop playing games and tell us the truth," Jeremy said angrily.

"I am!" Courtney, now in tears, shouted.

Jeremy and I exchanged a glance.

"I don't believe you," I said to Courtney. "You can be very convincing."

I thought about how she convinced me to go exploring in the woods. How terrified she was when we discovered Amara's body down in that abandoned basement. Then my thoughts went to Jeremy. How he even said his acting skills were phenomenal. He had tricked me too. I had believed his shock when I told him about the abandoned house. The way he was lying to everyone, the police, and his mom. How he kept his relationship with Courtney a secret from me for so long.

"Actually, you both can be," I said, backing away from both of them. "How do I know you both aren't lying to me?" I asked. My head was spinning, and I knew one, if not both were lying to me right now. "I'm sick of the lies. Just tell me the truth. Tell me the truth now, or I'm calling the police and telling them everything." I was shouting at this point, and I didn't care who heard me. I just wanted the truth once and for all.

"Well, it wasn't me. I'll tell you that right now," Jeremy said. He was angry and glaring at Courtney. "It was you!" he said to her, stepping toward her quickly and grabbing her arms.

Courtney let out a pained cry. "It wasn't. Please let go of me, you're hurting me," she whimpered.

"No!" Jeremy shouted. "Cut your shit off right now! We're done playing."

I stepped towards Jeremy and grabbed his shoulder. "Let her go," I said, my heart racing with fear. I had never seen Jeremy so angry before. He'd never acted like that before. "I believe her," I whispered.

"I don't!" he said loudly, never taking his eyes or hands off Courtney, who was now trying to squirm her way out of his tight grip, tears flooding down her cheeks.

"Please, Jeremy," Courtney whimpered. I could see that she was in a lot of pain.

"Fine," Jeremy said, still angry. He released his grip on Courtney but didn't stop glaring at her. The hatred in his eyes and his anger was so intense that it made my stomach ball up and tears came to my eyes. "I'll let you go," he said.

Courtney rubbed her arms where Jeremy had gripped her. Tears continued to flood down her cheeks. As she turned to walk towards me, Jeremy lunged at her.

CHAPTER TWENTY-TWO

HE PUSHED her down with all the force he could, not holding back. I watched in horror as Courtney's face smacked into a large rock, and a loud thud filled my ears.

It happened so fast, and I didn't see it coming so I had no time to react, to try to stop her fall, or jump between Jeremy and her.

Jeremy and I stood there looking at Courtney. I was in too much shock to know what to do. After a moment, I looked at Jeremy who was still glaring at Courtney with intense anger in his eyes.

"I've been done with that bitch for a while," he said, without emotion.

"What?" I asked bewildered. I wasn't quite sure that I had heard what he had said correctly. If I had, well, it wasn't making much sense to me now.

"I wanted to break up with her for a while now," he continued. "When she caught on to what I wanted to do, she threatened to tell you." He looked away from Courtney's lifeless body and looked at me. "I didn't want to hurt you. She knew that I would never do anything to hurt you, and she used that to keep me in this messed up relationship.

"I helped her with Amara because she asked me to. She gave me no choice though. Not really, because she said if I didn't, she'd tell you about us, and blame Amara's death all on me. I told her not to tell you where Amara's body was. She did anyway." He paused to wipe away a tear that had come to his eye. "Please believe me, the last thing I wanted was to drag you into any of this. Or to hurt you. This was all just her game."

I looked away from him and down at Courtney's body lying motionless on the ground. A puddle of blood had quickly formed around her head. "What do we do now?" I asked. I knew I should've felt panic and worry, but everything had happened so quickly. My brain was still trying to process Jeremy's words. My brain and emotions just hadn't caught up.

Jeremy knelt down next to Courtney and placed two fingers on the side of her throat. After a few seconds he said, "I'm not sure if I still feel a heartbeat." He stood up and we stood there in silence.

"I think I have an idea," Jeremy said. I looked at him questioningly. He continued. "The police still think there's a killer on the loose. Let's drag her into the woods deeper and bury her there. They'll find her and blame it on the killer. We just won't say anything. Then we can finally forget any of this ever happened."

Before I could answer, my phone alerted me of a text message. I looked at Jeremy, scared as I grabbed my phone. "Who is it?" he asked.

"My mom," I answered. "She's letting me know that

she has to leave for a while. She has some errands to run. She'll be home in an hour. She wants me home quickly."

"So, we need to work fast," Jeremy said. He lifted Courtney and carried her in his arms. I followed him into the woods, anxiously looking around me to make sure no one else was around. After a few minutes, he stopped. "This is a good place." He set her down a little too carelessly.

"Should we just leave her and go?" I asked.

"No, I think we should try to bury her a little," he said.

"We don't have shovels," I said.

"We have our hands," Jeremy replied.

So, we spent the next 20 minutes or so digging up dirt with our hands. During that time, it started to rain. When Jeremy was satisfied, he placed her in the little nook sized hole we managed to quickly dig. Then we worked fast to throw dirt on top of her.

"Let's hurry back now," Jeremy said. "I told my mom the three of us were just going to get some sodas and snacks." He rubbed his dirty hands on his pants.

"How are you going to explain this?" I asked, gesturing to his dirty body.

"I fell in the dirt," he said.

We walked out of Kitney Park quickly. There was no one around, which we were grateful for. The last thing we needed were witnesses.

"What do we say about Courtney?" I asked before we split off to go our own ways to get home.

"The last time we saw her, she was walking towards her house?" he answered.

"How are you so good at this?" I asked.

"At what?"

"At coming up with these explanations off the top of your head?" I truly wondered how he could just come up with a lie so easily.

"I don't know," he replied. "But I'm happy I can."

I needed to get home quickly. I could smell the wet concrete, the dank, dark sky above me promising another downpour, and soon. I quickened my pace to try to beat the rain, and my mom, to the house. I was soaking wet, and muddy. I didn't want to have to explain to her the reason why.

At least the job was done, for now. Unless someone went digging and made the discovery.

I can't believe this all started out with a dare.

CHAPTER TWENTY-THREE

"AND WE DID FIND COURTNEY," Detective Miller stated, spreading his fingers out wide on the table in front of him. "But my question now is, who sent the text to Jeremy and Courtney?" He looked Neve dead in the eyes and asked, "Was it you?"

Neve sat upright, looking serious and answered the detective's question. "No, it wasn't." When the detective squinted an eye at her as if to say, 'Sure, it wasn't', Neve added, "I'm telling nothing but the truth here."

Neve leaned forward and folded her hands in front of her on the table. "Jeremy sent the message to Courtney and himself," she stated.

"Why would he do that?" the detective asked, furrowing his dark eyebrows.

"His motive from the very beginning was to set up Courtney, to get rid of her," Neve explained. "He really did want out of the relationship."

"But why kill her?" the detective asked, leaning back, now, in his seat. "And why involve you?"

"I want to believe that he didn't mean to kill her. I really do." *Neve looked down, the memory of watching Jeremy attack Courtney and watching as she fell to her death saddened her.*

Looking back up at the detective, Neve added, "I think he wanted me to be there as part of the set up on Courtney. Maybe he knew that I would take his side. Also, I think he just really wanted me to know the truth. At least that's what I am hoping for."

"The way you described what happened, it sounds like he had no remorse whatsoever over killing Courtney."

"He didn't," Neve stated.

"He was so quick to take her out and bury her." The detective leaned forward. "Almost like he planned this. Meditated on how everything would happen."

"It does seem that way."

"So, how did you find out that it was Jeremy who sent the message?" The detective asked.

Then

After Jeremy and I had separated, I headed straight home. I was muddy, wet, and cold, cold to my core. I couldn't believe what had just happened, almost like a nightmare, a real living nightmare. I remembered thinking, *'How did my life come to this? It almost doesn't feel real. This can't be real life!'*

I entered my house, grateful that my mom was still out, and I could shower and clean up before she returned. Once I entered the bathroom and peeled off my muddy, damp clothes, I put them in a pile behind the bathroom door. *I need to wash those before anyone sees them!*

In the shower, I let the scalding hot water rush over me, taking with it the mud and dirt. Too bad it couldn't take away everything that had happened in the past two days and bring back Courtney.

The tears I had been holding in streamed down my face, and once they started, they didn't stop. I don't know just how long I had been crying, standing there under the hot water, but I was startled back to reality by my bathroom door opening.

"Oh, thank God you're home." It was my mom. "I've been calling you. I was so worried when you didn't answer. I had thought maybe something happened. I rushed home as fast as I could."

"Sorry, Mom," I said. "I got caught up in the rain and wanted to shower. My phone must be in my room, that's why I didn't hear you calling."

My mom gasped. "Neve, what happened? Why are your clothes all muddy?" she asked, sounding concerned.

Her question threw me off. I hadn't planned on her arriving back home before I washed my clothes. I said the first thing that popped into my mind. "I slipped and fell in some mud. I'll wash them when I am all finished in here." *Jeremy's excuse came in handy.*

"Oh, I'll do them. You've been through so much the past few days. Just get some rest," she said. I could hear her picking up my clothes. "I'll make us something to eat, okay?"

"Thanks, Mom," I responded. She left as I got out of the shower. I was relieved that she bought my story. I quickly dried myself and got dressed. I wanted to lie down for a few minutes before my mom called me downstairs to eat something. She would want to talk, but I wasn't ready to talk again. I feared that the true story would fall out. *What would happen if it did?*

I tried to get that thought out of my head as I curled onto my bed. I reminded myself of all the reasons I couldn't speak the truth. But, as much as I tried, I couldn't keep it from gnawing away at my brain. *Telling so many lies is really starting to mess with me.* Replaying everything that had happened over the last few days, I imagined the lies taking place instead of the actual events, hoping to convince myself the lies were true and that all the made-up things actually happened.

Then, a burning question popped into my head.

CHAPTER TWENTY-FOUR

"WHO SENT that last text to Jeremy and Courtney?" I said out loud, to nobody in particular. The question burned through my brain. I knew it wouldn't stop until it was answered.

I remembered Courtney crying, pleading with Jeremy, and me, that it wasn't her who sent the message. That she really had deleted the app that could make a phone number anonymous. She was so convincing. Too convincing maybe. But were her tears real? Or was it another one of her acts?

If it wasn't Courtney, then that would leave Jeremy. I reached for my phone to call him, but hesitated before hitting send. I remembered the look in his eyes. Pure anger. It made him unrecognizable to me. I wondered if he would be angry at me for asking if it was him who sent the message again.

I heard my mom calling for me from the kitchen. Setting my phone back down on the bed, I headed downstairs, calling Jeremy would have to wait.

My mom made lunch for the two of us, tuna sandwiches. We sat in silence, no questions asked, no talking at all. The silence was exactly what I wanted, needed, right now. I think she sensed that I needed this breathing moment to just indulge without worrying about everything going on around us. I was still trying to convince myself of all the lies, and it was getting harder for me to go along with the stories, *so if we were going to sit there in silence, I would take it!*

After we finished lunch, I headed back up to my room to finally call Jeremy. I knew I had to make this call because I needed the truth, once and for all. I knew I wouldn't think about anything else until I did.

After two rings, Jeremy answered, "Neve, what's wrong?"

"Can you talk right now?" I asked.

"Hold on," he replied. I heard a muffled voice, and after a few seconds, he spoke again. "Sorry, I had to tell my mom you wanted to talk. What's going on?"

"I haven't been able to stop thinking about everything, so I had to call and ask you something," I started, with a shaky voice. "Who sent the message? You know, the last anonymous message that you and Courtney both got?"

Silence. My insides twisted with anxiety as I waited for him to respond, and when he didn't, I went on. "It's just, well, Courtney said she didn't. The way she was crying. I just, I don't know."

More silence, and then, "Damn, Neve, you're still siding with her, after everything she has put you through? After how she constantly treated you?" He was angry. I could tell by the way his voice was strained that he was trying to stay quiet, to not raise his voice.

I didn't know what to say, because I didn't know what to believe anymore. *No one was who I had thought them to be or who I had known them to be.* All I could finally manage to say was, "I don't know."

"God, I guess it doesn't matter anymore." He sighed, still clearly angry but concealing it well enough. "I sent the damn message."

"Why? Why did you send it?" I said stunned and confused. *How could he do this?*

"I needed this to be over. I knew she would get the message, see that I had the message then call you to see if you got it too. It all worked the way I wanted it to."

I gasped, his words shook me. "You wanted to kill Courtney?" I asked, dumbfounded.

"I didn't." He paused before continuing. "I mean, yeah, I've thought about it. Tell me you haven't."

"No," I said. That was the truth. I never wanted to see Courtney dead, no matter what she said or did to hurt me. I just wanted her to move or stop talking to me. *I have never wished death upon anyone!*

"Well… I did," he said while pausing between words, his voice once again strained with anger. "I didn't think she would actually die when I pushed her. I just wanted to knock her out. I wanted–" His voice was cut off by muffled voices in the background.

"Sorry, that was my mom," Jeremy said to me after a moment. "They found Courtney. She's alive, but in bad shape." Then the line went dead.

CHAPTER TWENTY-FIVE

I RAN to tell my mom about Courtney, leaving out the truth. "The murderer must've snatched her on her way to her house," I explained to my shocked, worried mother. "They found her in the woods. She is barely alive." *I can't believe she's alive!*

Knowing that she had been found, my mind raced with anxiety and guilt. I felt horrible. With each lie I told, I found it getting easier. The lies seemed to just keep stacking up, but what choice did I have except to continue with the stories?

My mom drove me to the hospital where they'd taken Courtney. Jeremy and his mom were already there when we arrived. Courtney was alive, breathing, but barely hanging on. Jeremy and I sat beside her bed while our moms were in the hall comforting her parents, who were in tears and trying to understand why their daughter was unconscious in the hospital. *Do not look at them!*

Jeremy touched my arm and whispered, "I can't believe

this." His face looked solemn, and I wondered if that was just another act.

"What?" I said, loudly, forgetting that we were supposed to be whispering and that I was supposed to be beside myself with sadness. "That she's actually still alive?"

"Neve," Jeremy said, raising his eyebrows and gesturing towards the hallway where all of our unsuspecting parents were.

Before he could say anything, I stood up and walked into the hall. My mother wrapped me in a comforting hug. Looking over my mom's shoulder, I saw Jeremy placing his hand over Courtney's lifeless hand. It was disgusting to see him look so sad over her when all along he wanted to see her hurt, to see her dead.

All of the alarms from the machines Courtney was hooked up to suddenly started going off. Instantly there was a rush of doctors and nurses running past us and into her room, pushing and pulling all sorts of medical equipment in with them. "Code Blue" rang throughout the hospital. Jeremy was escorted out of the room by a large male nurse, and Courtney's parents watched their daughter from the hall, looking completely helpless.

A few minutes later, which felt like hours, two doctors came out and pulled Courtney's parents aside. I could faintly hear, "We're sorry. We did everything we could."

As the words left the doctor's mouth, Courtney's mom slid down the wall, sobbing loudly. Her husband, tears streaming down his face, wrapped his arms around his wife to keep her from falling to the floor.

The shock that echoed through me prevented me from realizing what had just happened. Once the realization that Courtney was dead hit me, I took off running. I heard my mother shouting for me to come back, but I couldn't stop. I needed to be away from everything, my own emotions included. I didn't stop running until I was at Kitney Park, where it all started.

Now

The Detective listened intently to everything Neve had said. He didn't look shocked by what he heard. His whole career was built on gruesome unbelievable stories that were reality to someone.

As soon as Neve stopped speaking, he said, "Sounds like he wanted you to know so he had someone to go down with him. An accomplice of sorts." He clasped his hands together and leaned forward to ask, "When was the last time you spoke with Jeremy?"

"That night," Neve answered. "I avoided him at school, and he wasn't too desperate to talk with me either. After we graduated, I left Kitney and never went back. I could never face what had happened that fall."

"But you never forgot?"

"Never," Neve confessed.

"So why say anything now?" the detective asked, intrigued.

"I needed to. To move on with my life. I thought if I could finally just say something, it would finally be over and stop haunting my every waking moment."

"Does it feel over?"

"As long as this memory lives within me, it will never be over." Neve sighed. "So what happens now?"

"Now we need to track down Jeremy Forester," Detective Miller answered. "You wouldn't know how we could contact him would you?"

"No," Neve responded quickly, sincerely. "Again, I haven't spoken to him since that last night, the night Courtney died."

"Not a single word?" the detective asked suspiciously. "You two shared all these secrets together and haven't spoken a word since that night at the hospital?"

"No," Neve said sternly, sitting straighter in her uncomfortable white plastic chair. "Once I left Kitney, I wanted to wash all of this away. Sure, he tried reaching out in the beginning, but I never responded to his messages or answered his calls. I ended up blocking his number and deleting it. I blocked him on all social media platforms. I'm sorry but I won't be able to help you track him down."

"Why?" the detective asked. "Why haven't you spoken to him?"

"It made me remember all that I've wanted to forget," Neve answered.

"Well, that's alright. You know we have the tools to be able to track him down, even without your help," the detective said, before exiting the room, leaving Neve alone to wonder about what would happen after they found him.

CHAPTER TWENTY-SIX

THE DETECTIVE HAD BEEN GONE *for a long time, at least it seemed that way to Neve. She refused to look at the clock that hung on the wall in the far corner of the room across from her, nor did she pull her phone from her purse beside her on the floor. Checking the time would just make it pass more slowly, and she wanted time to fly by. The anticipation of events to come was unbearable.*

What she dreaded most was facing Jeremy, and the person he truly was scared her deep in her core.

Finally, the detective walked back in. He set a Styrofoam cup of steaming black coffee in front of her. "You can go to the break room just down the hall for cream," he told her, pointing in the direction of the break room. "Help yourself to any snacks in there. You're going to be here for a while. We tracked down Jeremy Forester. He's on his way here."

The Detective left Neve to drink her coffee, leaving the door open on his way out, so she could enter and exit the room freely, however, she was asked not to leave the station. She was being held for more questioning.

She couldn't push herself to leave the room. She just sat there staring into her cup of coffee. She tried to imagine the questioning that would happen. She pictured Jeremy being arrested and wondered if that would finally put her guilt to rest. If the stress she felt carrying the weight of these secrets would just vanish once justice was served.

It was probably about a half hour later when Jeremy arrived. Detective Miller escorted him into the questioning room. He was asked to take a seat beside Neve. The detective stepped out, saying he had to take a call, but that he would return quickly.

Neve watched as Jeremy took his seat, worry written all over his face, then she went right back to staring into her coffee.

"I swear, Neve, I didn't say a word to anyone," Jeremy whispered into her ear.

"It was me, Jeremy. I told them the truth," Neve whispered back cautiously, bracing in preparation for Jeremy's anger.

"You did what!?" Jeremy asked, astonished.

The Detective walked in and spoke to Jeremy. "We have some questions we need you to answer. Remember, please be honest. We already got a full account testimony from Ms. Anderson."

"Okay, no problem," Jeremy said, scooting in his chair.

"Did you attempt to kill Courtney Scott?"

"No," Jeremy said, confused.

"It'll be easier if you give us full cooperation."

"I am cooperating. I didn't attempt to kill Courtney. I loved her," Jeremy said, sounding heart broken. "Wait, is that what she told you?"

The detective looked from Neve to Jeremy before standing to open the door. "Ms. Anderson, would you mind taking a seat in the lobby?"

Neve got up, obediently, and went to sit in the lobby.

Neve stayed in the lobby for several hours while the detective went back to question Jeremy alone. She wondered why Jeremy was still sticking to the lie. She thought it was probably because he didn't want to get arrested.

When the Detective appeared again, Jeremy was following closely behind him. Neve and Jeremy switched spots in the lobby, and Neve was brought back into the room for more questioning.

Once back in the room with the door closed, they took their same seats across from each other. The detective cleared his throat and asked, "Is there anything you want to add to your testimony?"

"No, I told you everything," Neve answered.

"Well, Jeremy tells us a different story. He also has video proof for some things he told me, proof that lines up with his story." Neve opened her eyes wide in disbelief. "Well, what did he tell you?"

"You killed Amara and drug her body to that abandoned house. It was actually you who convinced Courtney to explore Kitney woods that night. When Jeremy tried to stop you from burying Amara in the middle of the woods, you attacked him. And lastly, you were the one who killed Courtney." The detective leaned forward over the table. "Would you like me to go on?"

"You said he has proof of this? I would like to see this proof."

The detective pulled a phone from his pocket. It was an old phone of Jeremy's from years ago. He played a video of a younger Neve standing in Kitney woods, saying, "No one will know about this. I can flip this whole thing to make you guys go down for this." The phone was held at Jeremy's side. The movements were shaky, but there was no denying the glimpses of

Neve standing across from him. The rest of the video was Neve telling them the kidnapping and attack story and making Courtney and Jeremy swear to stick to it.

The video released a flood of memories in Neve's mind. She saw herself attack Amara. She saw herself dragging Amara from the basement in Old Kitney woods and burying her in the wet ground. Tears streamed down Neve's face.

"What's happening to me?" Neve cried.

"My best guess is that you started to believe your own lies. You turned those lies into memories. Those lies drove you to insanity. They ate at you and made you confess. Good thing Jeremy brought in that footage, or the wrong person might've gone down for your crimes. Would you like to hear your confession about killing Courtney too? It's a voice recording from the hospital." The detective held up Jeremy's old phone. "It's all on here. I asked him why he didn't come forward with all this footage before, but he said he was scared of you, and for you. My guess is he'll be in a lot of trouble as well."

Neve shook her head no, tears streaming down her face as realization hit her. Memory after memory flooded her brain, exploding out of the recesses of her mind after being locked away and replaced for so long.

EPILOGUE

6 YEARS Later

It took nearly a year and a half for the jury to decide I was guilty on two counts of murder and for the judge to decide that I wasn't mentally fit for prison. I was sent to a criminal institution, where I spent most of my time heavily medicated and isolated.

After the first three years, the doctors decided they would try to rehabilitate me by weaning me off the meds and allowing me small increments of time around other patients in what they called 'general population'. *That didn't work out.*

Weaning me from the meds was the worst thing the doctors could've done. The medication kept me from remembering everything. When all the memories flooded back, I went completely berserk. During lunch one day, I had what the doctor referred to as an episode. I threw a tray across the cafeteria, hitting another patient and leaving a small mark on her arm. The memory of what I'd done to Amara triggered that episode. After that, the doctors were on high alert. I was, again, placed in an isolation area, meds promptly administered. *Finally, I am able to forget again!*

After the detective showed me the video on the phone that Jeremy brought on the night of my confession, my delusional world I had created for myself completely dissipated. The doctors say it's because my mind couldn't handle the trauma of what I'd done.

My mom visited me all the time at first, but me being a human zombie made her sad. The visits decreased to only holidays, but she did write to me every week. I disregarded the letters, they triggered memories that the meds couldn't conceal. Memories of a normal happy life. Those memories made me upset, and having those feelings of being down while in this place was unbearable.

I would remain institutionalized until I could be deemed fit to serve time in prison.

Jeremy was charged for withholding information, making him an accomplice to my crimes. He was sentenced to eight years in prison with no possibility of parole. The life he had built for himself was destroyed. After high school, he'd gone on to become a math teacher. His students loved him, the school faculty spoke highly of him, that is until they found out the secrets he harbored.

He was also engaged, and he and his fiance were ready to start their life together and have a family of their own. It was unknown if she remained by his side, but at the trial she looked tense and angry. During a few of the court recesses, people could hear them arguing, though they tried their best to be quiet. She walked out of the courthouse one day and didn't return to any of his hearings after.

His own mom stopped speaking to him. She couldn't believe that the respectable young man she raised, the one she believed would always do the right thing, didn't confess.

In the end, Jeremy felt a lot of regret throughout the years for withholding their secrets for so long. The truth had been eating him alive. He had tried to forget, to pretend he didn't hold the knowledge of what had happened all those years ago. No matter how hard he tried to avoid it, to hide it away, it all came out anyway. The truth always gets revealed, no matter what.

ACKNOWLEDGMENTS

I would like to acknowledge and thank beth hudson, ink., Mint2Be, and Amanda Johnson. This team of people and all the love and hard work behind the scenes is what made this book possible, and to them I will always be grateful.

To my friends on TikTok, thank you for hyping me up with your excitement for The Dare, it's what has kept me going. You all are the very best!

ABOUT THE AUTHOR

Ava Stone is a mother of two wildly creative and funny children. She is, and always will be, a bookworm at heart. She has been writing fictional stories since elementary school. She has even won writing contests throughout her academic years.

While she loves to read everything, thriller and horror will always be her passion and favorite genres.

www.ingramcontent.com/pod-product-compliance
Lightning Source LLC
Chambersburg PA
CBHW022129150726
47992CB00002B/515